THE RANCHER
AND THE BABY

Elizabeth August

P9-CRH-126

Published by Silhouette Books
America's Publisher of Contemporary Romance

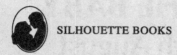

SILHOUETTE BOOKS

ISBN 0-373-65342-5

THE RANCHER AND THE BABY

This edition published by arrangement with Harlequin Books S.A.

® and TM are trademarks of Harlequin Books S.A., used under license. Trademarks indicated with ® are registered in the United States Patent and Trademark Office, the Canadian Trade Marks Office and in other countries.

Visit Silhouette Books at www.eHarlequin.com

Printed in U.S.A.

ELIZABETH AUGUST

lives in the mountains of North Carolina with her husband, Doug. Her three sons are now grown and have left home in pursuit of their careers. She and her husband are playing more golf and bridge, and Doug's game is improving. Elizabeth is enjoying being outdoors and she loves the beauty of the golf courses. As a cancer survivor she plays in tournaments that support cancer research and wishes to send out her very deepest wishes to all of her readers who have survived and those who are now fighting the various forms of this disease.

Please address questions and book requests to:
Silhouette Reader Service
U.S.: 3010 Walden Ave., P.O. Box 1325, Buffalo, NY 14269
Canadian: P.O. Box 609, Fort Erie, Ont. L2A 5X3

To Donnie and Juanita,
whose love and kindness
bring joy to the hearts of others.

ELIZABETH AUGUST

lives in the mountains of North Carolina with her husband, Doug. Her three sons are now grown and have left home in pursuit of their careers. She and her husband are playing more golf and bridge, and Doug's game is improving. Elizabeth is enjoying being outdoors and she loves the beauty of the golf courses. As a cancer survivor she plays in tournaments that support cancer research and wishes to send out her very deepest wishes to all of her readers who have survived and those who are now fighting the various forms of this disease.

Please address questions and book requests to:
Silhouette Reader Service
U.S.: 3010 Walden Ave., P.O. Box 1325, Buffalo, NY 14269
Canadian: P.O. Box 609, Fort Erie, Ont. L2A 5X3

To Donnie and Juanita,
whose love and kindness
bring joy to the hearts of others.

same cloth as his father. Family was important to him. And, in this case, Dalton had added motivation.

A curl of guilt tormented her. Ignoring it, she turned to the picture of a handsome, brown-eyed, brown-haired, smiling young man on the mantel. "No one could be a better protector for your child than Dalton," she addressed the photo. "If Miss Varden is a good mother, she has nothing to worry about. But if she has neglected my grandson or caused him harm in any way, I would not want to be in her shoes when Dalton finds her."

Amelia Varden wiggled her toes to get the threatening cramps out of her feet and sighed. The lunchtime rush was over. Nearly all the customers were now gone, the tables were bused and she could relax for a while. She was just about to pour herself a cup of coffee when the bell over the door sounded, accompanied by a gust of frigid January air. Silently she groaned and put the cup aside.

"Now if I was twenty years younger..." Bessy McHaggen, the owner of the diner in which Amelia worked, let the sentence dangle unfinished.

Amelia looked toward the door to see who had caused the mischievous glimmer in Bessy's eyes. The source of her employer's admiration was a tall, dark, rugged-looking man wearing jeans, Western boots, a Stetson and a heavy sheepskin coat. Amelia judged him to be somewhere in his early thirties.

"Now there's a sign of good manners," Bessy added with a pleased smile as the man took off the hat and nodded a polite greeting to the two women. "Not the most handsome man I've ever seen but I prefer that world-weary look myself." Bessy's grin of appreciation broadened. "Nice build, too," she noted, watching him remove his coat before he took a seat in one of the booths. "Not too muscle-bound, broad shoulders, flat abdomen. Moves like a man in good physical condition."

Amelia had to admit the stranger appeared to be a healthy specimen. "He's probably married."

"No ring," Bessy observed candidly.

"That doesn't mean a thing."

Bessy frowned. "You're much too young to be so cynical."

"I watched a friend of mine learn life's lessons the hard way."

"Guess you've learned a few that way yourself." Bessy smiled. "But you can't let the past stop you from having a future."

"What I'm concerned about right now is my tip. If I don't get a menu to that man, he might figure service here is too slow and leave."

"Now that would be a shame." Bessy again glanced appreciatively toward the newcomer. "He reminds me of my third husband."

"The rodeo rider? The one who left you broke and stranded in Phoenix?" Amelia asked dryly.

"I guess I'm one of those people who's always open to new lessons no matter how hard," Bessy returned with a laugh that said she'd enjoyed her life, the bumps and all.

Bessy was welcome to her adventures, Amelia thought as she left the kitchen. As for herself, all she wanted was a quiet, peaceful existence.

"The special today is roast beef and gravy with mashed potatoes and peas," she said politely. Handing the man a menu, she noticed that his hands were calloused. Obviously he hadn't developed his muscles simply working out in a gym.

His gaze flickered over her, then came to rest on her face. "Is it any good?" he asked in an easy Western drawl. In spite of his friendly manner, there was a coldness in his eyes.

Clearly, he hadn't been impressed by his inspection, she decided. And that was fine with her. Still, she experienced a small sting of insult. She knew she wasn't a raving beauty, but her raven hair coupled with green eyes and features that fitted well together usually garnered, at least, a friendly glimmer from male customers.

"Everything I cook is good," Bessy yelled through the serving window.

Peering around Amelia to the wiry, gray-haired woman, the man smiled stiffly. "I learned a long time ago never to anger the cook." He returned his attention to Amelia. "I'll take the special and a cup of coffee."

She noticed that his eyes had softened some when he'd looked toward Bessy, then hardened again when he'd placed his order. Maybe he's afraid I'll fling myself at him if he gives me the least bit of encouragement, she thought wryly. What an ego some men had! "Right away," she replied crisply, her tone letting him know he was safe from her.

"Hey, Sweet Lips, we could use some more coffee over here," a male voice called out as she headed back to the kitchen.

Bessy glared at the blond-haired, blue-eyed trucker seated in a corner booth with a buddy. "Her name's Amelia, Mike Johnson, and don't you forget it. You treat my waitresses with respect or get out!"

Mike grinned, giving a boyishness to his handsome features. "Yes, ma'am. You sure do look cute when you get riled, Miss Bessy."

Amelia knew Mike was just joking around. He and Bessy played out this scene at least once a week. Still, she didn't like the insinuation in his voice that she was a loose woman. She glanced to the stranger and caught a flicker of disapproval in his eyes. This wasn't the first time Mike had embarrassed her, but it would be the last, she vowed. Carrying the pot of coffee over to his table, she paused and her eyes narrowed threateningly. "Next time the coffee will end up in your lap," she warned him.

ELIZABETH AUGUST   13

"Okay, okay." He held up his hands and his expression became serious. "But you do have kissable-looking lips, and I've been thinking that instant fatherhood wouldn't be so bad. How about if you and I take in a movie...get to know each other?"

As if on cue, a child's cry erupted from the back room.

"You sure you want someone else's rug rat interrupting your own bid for fatherhood?" Bruce Collin, the second man at the table, asked with a laugh.

Mike's gaze traveled over Amelia appraisingly. "It might be worth it."

"Don't burn up any brain cells thinking too hard on it," Amelia said over her shoulder, already heading toward the cry. "You're never going to get a chance to find out."

Bruce let out a low whistle at her departing back. "Even I'm tempted," he admitted.

Her embarrassment at having the stranger privy to this exchange lingered. She told herself whatever he thought didn't matter. Still, she glanced toward him, wondering what his reaction would be. But he wasn't looking her way. Instead he was frowning in the direction from which a second baby's cry was coming.

Abruptly his gaze swung to her. There was accusation there, as if he felt she was neglecting an important duty. Her jaw tensed defensively. What right did he have to judge her?

"I'll serve the special," Bessy said, coming out of the kitchen carrying a plate and cup of coffee.

Amelia gave her a grateful smile and hurried past her. Her destination was the room beyond the kitchen that served as the living room of the small apartment built onto the diner. Through the open door, she saw her son standing, clutching the side of his playpen still groggy from his nap.

Seeing her, he smiled. "Mommy."

Suddenly everything was forgotten—the judgmental stranger, Bruce and Mike's lecherous flirting, even her tired feet. Lifting him up into her arms, she nuzzled his neck and hugged him. A warm glow of joy spread through her. There were times, she admitted, when raising Mitch was tough, but she could not imagine her life without him. He'd filled a void within her and she loved him with all her heart. "Did you sleep good?" she asked, laying him down on a blanket on the rug and beginning the task of changing his diaper.

He began to babble, the expression on his face serious, as if he were telling her something very important.

She caught the word *teddy* and knew he was talking about the stuffed bear he refused to sleep without. Perhaps in his dreams he and "teddy" had had an adventure, she mused. "Now that is interesting," she humored him.

His expression remaining serious, he continued to

rattle on while she finished changing his diaper and completed dressing him.

"How about some juice?" she asked as he scampered to his feet.

"Uce!" he agreed enthusiastically.

"Uce, it is." Grinning, she stood and offered him her hand.

Grabbing hold of a finger, he walked with her out into the diner. To Amelia's relief the two truckers were gone and their table had been bused.

"Here's your tip." Bessy slipped some dollar bills into the pocket of Amelia's apron. "And you deserve every cent of it for putting up with those two." The proprietress turned her attention to the child. "And how is my little man today? I heard you in there sawing logs."

Again Mitch burbled a slur of sounds.

Bending over, Bessy gave him a hug, then straightened. "I'm going to sit and have a bite." Putting action to her words, she sat down at the table closest to the kitchen door. A plate of the daily special was already there along with a cup of coffee. "Are you two going to join me?"

"I was going to give Mitch some juice and his midafternoon snack." Amelia pulled over a high chair and sat her son in it. Out of the corner of her eye, she glanced toward the stranger's table. There was a newspaper in his hands. Clearly he'd been reading while he ate, but now his attention was on her and her son. She was certain Bessy was taking good care of him, but pride caused her to want to make certain he had nothing to complain about where service was concerned. Making certain Mitch was securely strapped in, she said, ''Be back in a minute.''

Picking up the pot of coffee on her way, she headed to the man's table. ''More coffee?'' she offered.

He nodded his acceptance. ''Cute kid.''

''I think so,'' she replied.

''Takes after his father.''

The panic Amelia kept deeply buried threatened to surface. He's just making an observation, she chided herself. It would be a natural assumption that Mitch looked like his father. With his brownish-blond hair and brown eyes, he looked almost nothing like her. ''Yes, he does,'' she admitted. Wanting to turn the subject away from her child, she asked, ''Would you like some dessert?''

''That apple pie on the counter looks good. Is it homemade?''

''Made it fresh yesterday,'' Bessy called over her shoulder.

Not much said in this place missed her boss's ears, Amelia noted.

''In that case, I'll have a slice,'' the stranger said.

Relieved when he turned his attention back to his newspaper, Amelia had to admit he had an unnerving effect on her. It was the way he looked at her, cold and calculating, as if sizing her up like an opponent in a battle. Again she wondered if his ego was so big that he was worried about her throwing herself at him.

If so, he's living in a dreamworld, she mused as she cut his pie and poured some juice for her son. Pausing to hand Mitch his plastic mug of juice, she felt a prickling on her neck. Glancing over her shoulder, she saw the stranger again looking her way.

If she'd blown her tip because she'd taken a second to tend her son, so be it, she thought as she continued across the diner and served the pie. The man wasn't a local. She knew most of them by sight. Most likely he was just passing through town and they'd never see this particular customer in here a second time anyway. And that wouldn't bother her in the least.

Ignoring him, she returned to the table by the kitchen to find that Bessy had dished up two more ⌐es of the day's special for her and Mitch.

⌐r eat while we can,'' the proprietress re- ⌐monition, tying a large bib around

⌐lia ⌐t his meat into

fingers. "I've got to work on your table manners," she teased, watching him stuff a piece into his mouth.

He looked up at her with a questioning frown as if to say he couldn't understand what was so wrong in his method. Laughing lightly, she kissed him on the nose.

He crinkled his face and returned his attention to his food. Her own stomach growled, reminding her she hadn't eaten since early this morning. Knowing customers could walk in at any moment, she, too, applied herself to her food.

Halfway through her meal, she noticed that the stranger was still there. Excusing herself, she went to pour him more coffee. He was working the crossword puzzle. Obviously he'd come in to kill some time. Normally, she would have entertained herself by wondering who or what he was waiting for. But in his case, she just wished he'd leave.

She frowned at herself as she poured Bessy another cup of coffee before returning the pot to the warmer. Her attitude toward the stranger wasn't her. She usually felt an empathy for those in alone. If there was one thi understood, it was lonelin

It suddenly

pla

...Bee her da

peated her neck.

Mitch's she was right, Amena cu

Knowing pieces and a half, Mitch could use a spoon

tiny pieces and he did use it for the-potatoes

At a year, effectively, but the meat he preferred to use his

fairly peas, but for

nd peas.

...ly dawned on her that he didn't strike her as being lonely. He struck her as a man with her pose. Whatever his business is, it's none of mine, she told herself, shoving him out of her mind.

Mitch was sated and bored with his food by the

She

ress.

time she seated herself once again. Bessy had finished her meal and was cleaning him up. "You sit and eat," the older woman ordered. "I can't have my waitresses fainting from lack of food. Helen called while you were in getting Mitch up. She's got the flu now, too. I know it's going to be exhausting and I hate asking this, but I need you to stay and wait tables for the dinner crowd. And you'll be on your own."

Amelia forced a smile. Today she'd been on the breakfast and lunch shift. Right now she should be looking forward to going home. But she owed too much to Bessy to complain. Not very many employers would allow an employee to bring a child to work and, even more, use the employer's living room as a nursery during the busy hours. "Sure, no problem."

"Time for a little exercise," Bessy said, lifting Mitch out of the chair and putting him on the floor. "Now don't disturb the customers," she admonished.

He looked up at her, his expression serious, and again garbled sounds issued. The effect was to give the impression he was promising to obey. Then he toddled toward a box in the corner. From it he extracted a large truck and, on his hands and knees, began pushing the toy across the floor.

Bessy laughed. "Sam Riddly said he'd make a trucker out of him."

Amelia pictured the big, burly, white-haired

trucker who'd been courting Bessy for better than a year now. "Looks like he might be succeeding."

Bessy suddenly frowned. "Well, don't you let him. They're never home. My first husband was a trucker...always gone. That's why I'm not going to marry Sam. I want someone to keep me warm at night...every night." A speculative glimmer entered her eyes. "You could use a little companionship yourself. Have you noticed that Harry Wells has been coming in here real regular since his divorce?"

"I've noticed but I'm not interested," Amelia said firmly, hoping to discourage Bessy from doing any matchmaking.

"Doesn't light your fire, huh?"

"No, he doesn't." Amelia again felt a prickling on her neck. Out of the corner of her eye she saw the stranger watching her, his expression unreadable, and realized he'd been listening to her conversation. She couldn't entirely blame him for hearing. Bessy hadn't kept her voice low. Still, his eavesdropping irritated her. She tossed him a haughty glance that suggested he should mind his own business.

Frowning at himself as if angered by any show of interest in her, he returned his attention to the newspaper.

"Well, you should be looking for someone who ignites a few sparks," Bessy persisted, her voice taking on a motherly tone. "I know twenty-seven isn't all that old, but you're not getting any younger."

Amelia's attention returned to her employer. "I'm perfectly happy with my life as it is."

Bessy shook her head. "I'm all for a woman being independent and able to take care of herself. But I've never found a good substitute for a man to keep my feet warm at night."

"A heavy pair of socks works real well," Amelia assured her. Determined to end this conversation, she rose and carried her dishes to the kitchen.

When she returned, she discovered Mitch had found the stranger. He was standing about three feet from the man's table, staring at him.

Amelia was certain the man would send her son scurrying with a "get lost" look. Instead he nodded toward the boy in greeting. "The name's Dalton."

"Itch," the toddler responded, pointing a finger at himself.

"Glad to meet you, Mitch," Dalton replied.

He hadn't smiled, but the tone of his voice made his words sound genuine. Still, she didn't like her son making friends with strangers.

"Sorry he bothered you," she said, quickly crossing the room and lifting Mitch into her arms.

"No bother," the man who had introduced himself as Dalton replied in an easy drawl.

He turned his attention back to the crossword and Amelia carried Mitch into the kitchen. She was a little surprised the man had gotten her son's name correct on the first try. Most people guessed Mitch was saying Rich. The man had probably heard Bessy addressing Mitch by name, she reasoned, angry with herself for even giving the matter a second thought.

The walls felt as if they were closing in on her. Knowing it was because of the stranger, she frowned at herself for letting him get on her nerves. He was certainly a lot less irritating than some other customers she'd waited on. Still, she felt tense and in need of some fresh air. "I thought I'd take Mitch out for a walk," she informed Bessy. "You said you had some letters you wanted mailed?"

"The stack's right over there." Bessy indicated the mail holder on the counter with a twist of her head.

Quickly, Amelia bundled up Mitch. Then, grabbing the mail on her way, she left. Outside, the frigid wind whipped around them and she clutched her son's hand more tightly. As she breathed in the cold, crisp air, her muscles began to relax. The reason her nerves had been so on edge suddenly dawned on her. Although he'd been discreet for the most part, she'd felt as if he'd been continuously studying her, not the way a man studied a woman who appealed to him but more like an object he wasn't certain he wanted to be anywhere near. "He should get a life," she muttered under her breath.

Reaching the mailbox on the corner, she glanced back and saw him leaving. She'd noticed that the only car parked in front of the diner was a rental.